In memory of my fabulous teacher,
Hilda Farwell
—M.P.

To Emma sweetie pie Louise
—K.G.

MOO WhO?

By Margie Palatini

Illustrated by Keith Graves

KATHERINE TEGEN BOOKS
An Imprint of HarperCollins Publishers

Hilda Mae Heifer was out to pasture, having a glorious field day. She did a little running. A little jumping. And a whole lot of singing. Oh boy, could Hilda let loose with the tra-la-las. She was extremely enthusiastic…just not always on key. Warnings were out: Cover your ears when Hilda hit a high note.

She was right in the middle of a wailing "*mi-mi-moo*"
when suddenly, from out of nowhere, a hard and
high-flying cow pie came hurtling straight for Hilda.

Whiz. Wham. *Klunk.*

It knocked her right on the noggin, and down she went. Yup. It was lights out for *Hilda Mae Heifer.*

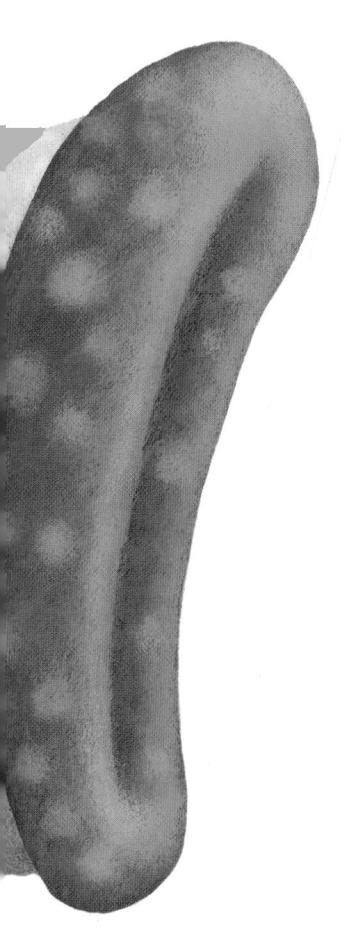

The poor girl came to a bit dazed, a tad dizzy, with a lump on her forehead so high you could play ringtoss... *and* without a clue of who she was— or what she did.

"Hu-u-u-h?" moaned Hilda.

Yes, it was sad but true—Hilda Mae Heifer had lost her moo.

A little woozy, a whole lot wobbly, and *very* confused, Hilda made her way over to a goose who was landing with a loud "Honk!"

"Honk," called Hilda.

"Honk. Honk. Honk!"

The goose looked at Hilda. "Are you honking at me?"

"Honk!" Hilda honked back.

"Lady, enough with that honking! You're a cow. You moo."

"Who?" answered Hilda. "Me? Moo?"

"Moo. Yes, that's what you do," said the goose. "Stop honking. You're not me."

"I'm not?" asked Hilda. The goose shook his head. "Well, just look at yourself.

"Do you have webbed feet?"
Hilda looked. No, she didn't.

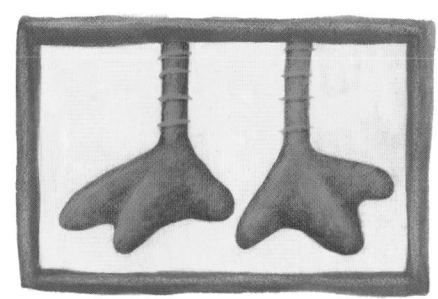

"Do you have two wings?"
Hilda looked. No, she did not.

"Do you fly to Canada every year?"
Hilda was quite certain she had
never flown to Canada, not even once.

"See?" he flapped. "You're no goose. You're a cow.
You moo."

Hilda gave it a try. "Moo-oo. Me? Moo?"

Hilda was not convinced that mooing was the thing she was supposed to be doing. That's when she heard some chicks cheeping and peeping with a mother hen.

"Peep," called Hilda.

"Peep. Peep. Peep!"

"Hey!" cried a chick. "Stop peeping at us!"

"Yes, stop that peeping immediately," said the mother hen. "You're no spring chicken. You're a cow. You moo."

"Who?" answered Hilda. "Me? Moo?"

"Moo. Yes, that's what you do. You're not a chicken."

"I'm not?" asked Hilda.
The chicken shook her head.
"Well, do you have feathers?"
Hilda looked. No, she didn't.

"Do you hunt and peck?"
No, Hilda did not do that either.

"Have you ever laid an egg before?"
No. And Hilda was very sure she
would have remembered doing that.
    "There you have it," clucked the hen.
"You're no chicken. You're a cow.
You moo."

So *Hilda* gave it another try.
"Moo-oo. Me? Moo?"
Hilda was still not convinced that mooing was what she should be doing.

That's when she saw a pig taking a mud bath. He gave out a loud squeal, snort, grunt, and oink. Hilda did the same.

"Pardon me, madam," said the pig. "But did you just *oink* at me?"

"Oink, oink. Oink!" answered Hilda.

"My dear," said the pig. "You're no swine. You're bovine. You moo."

"Who?" said Hilda. "Me? Moo?"

"Moo. Absolutely. That's what you do," said the pig. "You're a cow, not a sow."

"I am?" said Hilda.

"You're not ham," snorted the pig. "Why, do you have a curly tail?"

Hilda looked. No, she didn't.

"Are you pink and portly?"

Hilda looked. No, she wasn't.

"Are your relatives big boars?"

Hilda thought. Well…yes. Maybe that did describe some members of her family.

"Trust me," he grunted. "You're no pig. You're a cow. You moo."

Hilda gave it one more try. "Moo-oo. Me? Moo?"

Nope. Hilda still had no clue that what she was supposed to do was simply moo. It was not a very good feeling, not knowing what to say or do. And then Hilda saw a cat.

"Mew, mew, mew," the cat said to Hilda.

Hilda grinned with delight. "Mew too?"

"You mean, me and you? Heavens no," said the cat. "I mew. You moo."

"I do?" said Hilda.
"I really, really do?"

The cat nodded. "Good gracious, you're a cow, not a cat.

Do you have four paws?

HiSSSss!

Do you hiss?

A face full of whiskers?

Scratch?

RRRiiip!

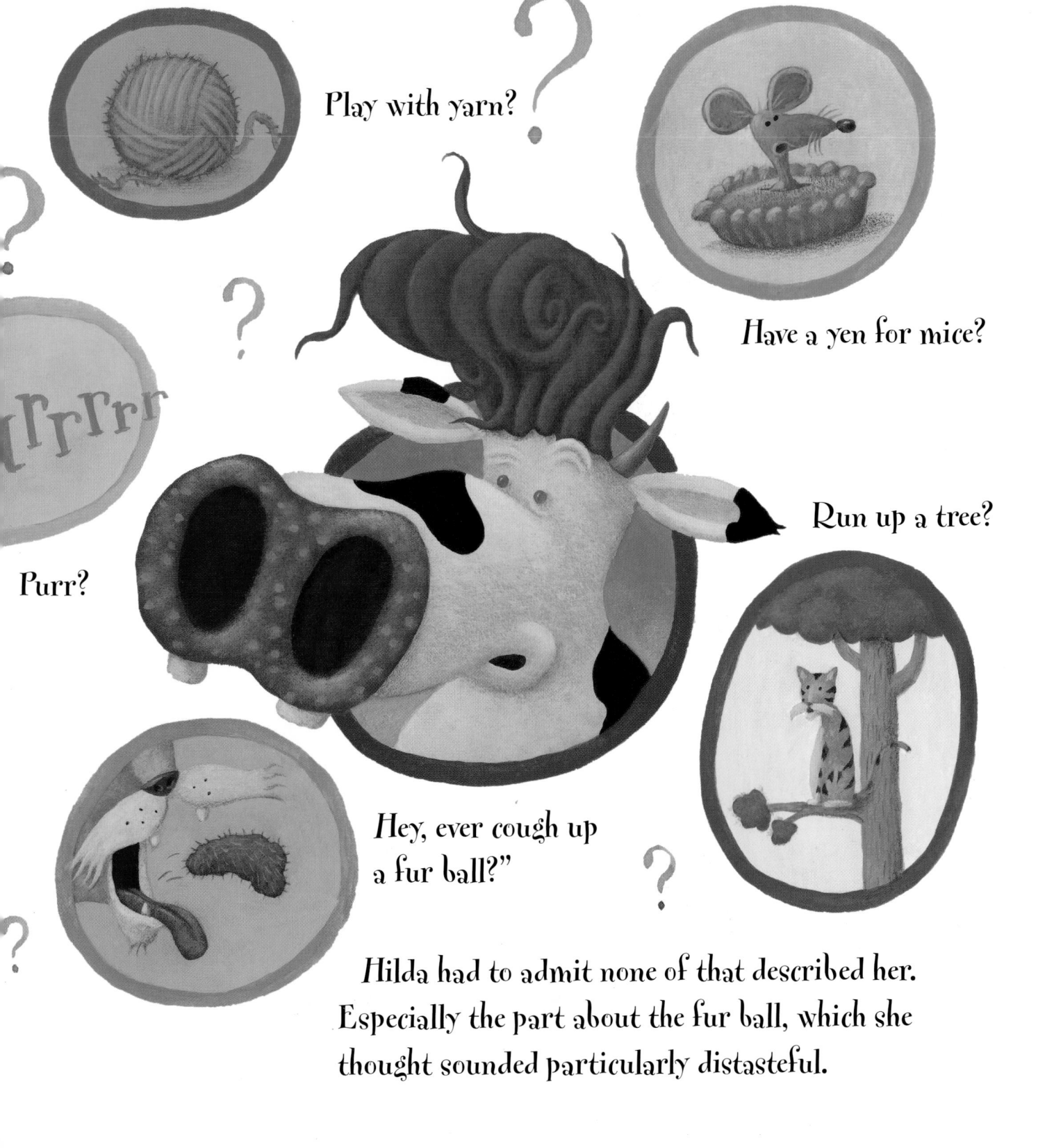

Play with yarn?

Have a yen for mice?

Purr?

Run up a tree?

Hey, ever cough up
a fur ball?"

Hilda had to admit none of that described her.
Especially the part about the fur ball, which she
thought sounded particularly distasteful.

"You are a cow," said the cat. "It's true. What you do is moo."

Hilda looked puzzled. "The goose **honks,** the chickens **peep,** the pig **oinks,** you **mew,** and I… **moo, moo, moo, moo?"**

"I think you've got it," said the cat. "Not mew, mew, mew. Moo. Moo. Moo."

"Moo-oo-ooo! Hmmm," said Hilda thoughtfully. There was something about that last moo that felt awfully familiar. "Moo-oooo-oooo," said Hilda again. "You know, I think perhaps I do."

So she did.
Hilda sang out with gusto.

"Mi m

ma

MOO. MOO. MOO. MOO. MOO.
mi mi. MOO. MOO. MOO. MOO.
Me! Moo! Mi, Moo. MOOOO-OOOO-OOO.
OO-MOO-MOO-MOO. MOO. MOO. MOO!"

Hilda grinned. "Who knew? I'm a cow—and how."
And that's how *Hilda Mae Heifer* got back her moo.

Everyone else got earplugs.